THE MYSTERY
OF THE
STOLEN BLUE PAINT

THE MYSTERY
OF THE
STOLEN BLUE PAINT

STORY AND PICTURES BY

STEVEN KELLOGG

Dial Books for Young Readers

New York

Dial Books for Young Readers
2 Park Avenue
New York, New York 10016

Published simultaneously in Canada by
Fitzhenry & Whiteside Limited, Toronto

Library of Congress Catalog Card Number: 81-15314
Printed in Hong Kong by South China Printing Co.
First Pied Piper Printing 1986
COBE
4   6   8   10   9   7   5   3

A Pied Piper Book is a registered trademark of
Dial Books for Young Readers,
a division of NAL Penguin Inc.,
®TM 1,163,686 and ®TM 1,054,312

THE MYSTERY OF THE STOLEN BLUE PAINT
is published in a hardcover edition by
Dial Books for Young Readers.
ISBN 0-8037-0285-x

*The art for each picture consists of a black
line-drawing and two halftone separations.*

To my wonderful sisters,
Barbara, Patti, and Martha

S.K.

There! My room is all fixed up. Come on, Homer. We'll take my paint and make a blue picture to hang over the desk.

Oh, no. Here comes my pesty cousin Jason.
Let's hide until he's gone.

Hi, Belinda. What are you and Homer doing
under this bush? Playing cops and robbers?
Can I play too?

No. I'm on my way to paint pictures.

Wouldn't you rather read to me?

Not now, Jason. Why don't you find
Simon and LouAnne and play with them?

Hi, Belinda. Simon and LouAnne and I have come to paint pictures with you.

I have only one little jar of blue paint.
There isn't enough for four artists.
But if you go play for a while, I'll come over
and read you your book later.

We'd rather stay here and watch you.

Well, all right. But don't bother me
while I'm painting.

Belinda, it's getting too windy!
Can't we go read now?

I told you I'd read later!

It's *not* too windy and I'm *not* through painting!

Crazy wind. I might as well give up
painting. I'll put my stuff away and read
that book to the little kids.

Hey! My blue paint is gone! And I know I still had a little bit left.

I'm sure they wouldn't have taken it.
It must have been one of those little kids.

This is a case for Inspector Belinda Baldini.

Jason! LouAnne! Simon! What happened
to my blue paint?

How would we know? We've been playing
inside ever since the windstorm came,
and you ran away without reading to us.

If the person who took my paint
doesn't confess right now, I'll never
read to anyone again, and there'll be big trouble
in this neighborhood.

I didn't do it, but maybe Simon did.
No, I didn't! What about Jason?
I bet it was LouAnne!
No, it wasn't!

Stop arguing and line up! I'll check each
of you for traces of blue paint.

Nothing but old chocolate ice cream,
peanut butter, clay, bubble gum, and dirt.
I'll bring my trusty police dog into the case.

Wake up, Homer. Which one of those
suspects took my blue paint?

Jason!

Hey! Homer has a blue tongue!

He's the guilty one! He ate my paint!

I guess I'm not a very good police inspector.

Okay, you were right and I was wrong.
But I'll make it up to you. Let's go up
to your apartment, and I'll read you as many
books as you want.